EXCERPTS FROM THE ENCYCLOPEDIA OF

UNDERWATER INVESTIGATIONS

ROB KOVITZ

A DROWNING

Offshore, a fisherman is tapping on lake ice
And calling to his son.
…
The fisherman, lifting his nets, whispers
A question to each pickerel, each pike.

W. D. Valgardson, A Drowning

INSTRUCTION MANUAL

There is a saying of the wise man: "When all things lay in the midst of silence then leapt there down into me from on high, from the royal throne, a secret word."

…

But, Sir, where is the silence and where the place in which the word is spoken?

Meister Eckhart, On Detachment

Gazarra opened the book. The first page swam with crooked, twisted, backwards-leaning letters.

"'Darkness was on the face of the deep,'" he began.

"I know," she told him. "I've been there."

David Homel, Get On Top

We all live in the same world's sea.
We cannot tell a story that leaves us
outside, and when I say *we*, I include
you. But in order to include you, I
feel that I cannot spend these pages
saying *I* to a second person.
Therefore let us say *he*, and stand
together looking at them.

George Bowering, Burning Water

The biggest secrets are the ones spread open before us.

Don Delillo, Underworld

THE DROWNER

Gimli—A 22-year-old Winnipeg man drowned Sunday afternoon at Gimli Beach after apparently suffering a seizure while swimming, police said.

Officials estimated more than 7,000 people were at the beach during the incident.

Two doctors on the scene, along with beach safety officers, applied CPR on the shore after family and friends pulled him out of the water, said RCMP Const. Jamie Slukynsky.

██████████████ was prone to seizures and disappeared under the water while swimming with a group of family and friends, he added.

He had been under water for several minutes before his companions found him and pulled him to shore, Slukynsky added.

An ambulance took ████ to Gimli General Hospital where he was pronounced dead, he added.

████'s is the 14th water-related death in the province so far this year.

Manitoba has Canada's highest per-capita rate of preventable water-related deaths. In 1995, 33 Manitobans drowned, seven in Lake Winnipeg alone.

Andrew Maxwell, Winnipeg Free Press

"So," he says, for want of anything better.

"I am an actress," she says, raising her chin a little, and looks it.

"I'm a drowner."

Robert Drewe, The Drowner

Robert G. Teather, *Encyclopedia of Underwater Investigations*

TAKE A DEEP BREATH

All right, let's put our cards on the table. I assure you I'm quite conscious of my position. Shall I tell you what it feels like? A man's drowning, choking, sinking by inches, till only his eyes are just above water.

Jean-Paul Sartre, No Exit

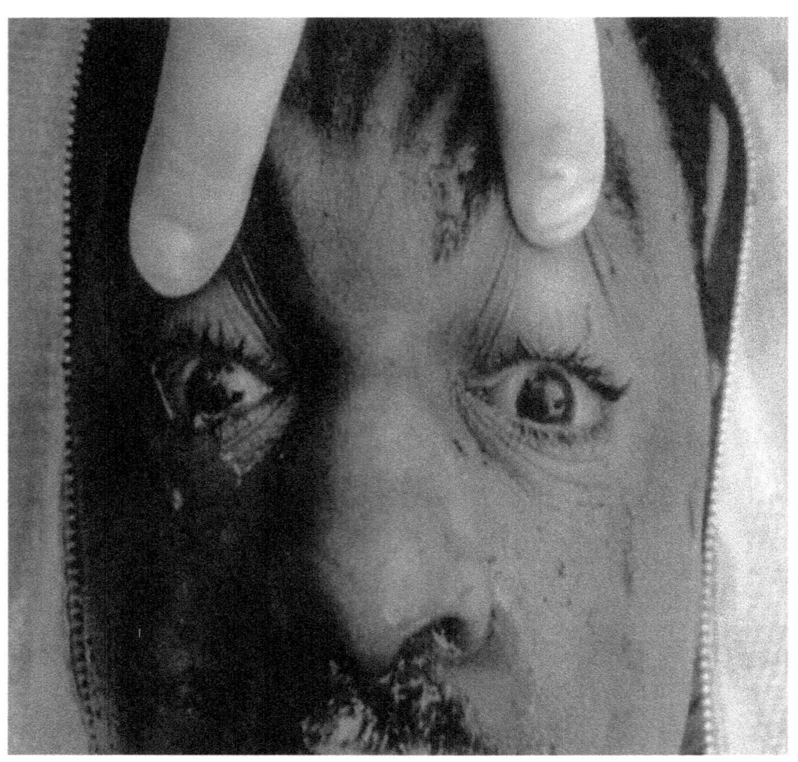

Unnoticed by his friends, who are now nearing the far shore, he slips quietly below the surface. Sinking slowly at first, he loses his ability to hold his breath and an ever-increasing carbon dioxide buildup forces his diaphragm to contract uncontrollably. A deep inspiration of water follows. With his lungs nearly empty, he has lost ten to fifteen pounds of buoyancy and he sinks faster. The water now in his lungs allows the carbon dioxide in his blood to leave quickly through the alveolar bed. His burning desire to breathe is now satisfied but the blood returning from his lungs to his heart has drastically changed its chemistry. His heart will not continue to function for very much longer.

Robert G. Teather, Encyclopedia of Underwater Investigations

> Lord, Lord! methought what pain it was to drown:
> What dreadful noise of water in mine ears!
> What sights of ugly death within mine eyes!
> Methought I saw a thousand fearful wracks;
> A thousand men that fishes gnaw'd upon.

William Shakespeare, Richard III

To get a better idea try this: focus on these words, and whatever you do don't let your eyes wander past the perimeter of this page. Now imagine just beyond your peripheral vision, maybe behind you, maybe to the side of you, maybe even in front of you, but right where you can't see it, something is quietly closing in on you, so quiet in fact you can only hear it as silence. Find those pockets without sound. That's where it is. Right at this moment. But don't look. Keep your eyes here. Now take a deep breath. Go ahead take an even deeper one.

Don't look.

I didn't.

Of course I looked.

Mark Z. Danielewski, House of Leaves

Robert G. Teather, *Encyclopedia of Underwater Investigations*

ASTOUNDED

Cold worlds shake from the oar.
The spirit of blackness is in us, it is in the fishes.
...
This is the silence of astounded souls.

Sylvia Plath, Crossing The Water

UNDERWATER CARPENTRY

Once I dropped acid three times a day for a month. It was the summer, my sixteenth. My family was taking our yearly vacation on Maui. I'd made this friend, Craig, a local surfer with great drug connections. Every morning we'd score a few blotter hits, hitch-hike to this remote beach, and spend the day zonked, hallucinating, babbling, and swimming around in the ocean. After several weeks, we started to lose it. We'd found this coral reef a short distance offshore. One day we robbed a hotel room, stole a truck, and transported the rooms's furnishings to the beach. We towed our loot, piece by piece, through the surf, underwater, and into this huge, cavelike nook in the reef, setting each chair, rug, et cetera, in place, then swimming furiously back for the surface. Our plan was to live in this cave, rent-free, far away from fascistic reality. It never crossed our minds that we wouldn't be able to breathe.

Dennis Cooper, Guide

        or better to become un-
astonished, your calmness showing
the misshapen's your home:
By a lake near Jasper a dozen scuba divers
circulated among dripping wooden chairs
set up in the sand.
           "Underwater carpentry"
a bystander explained—each spring
they take mallets and pegs into the lake
to see who can build the best chair.
When I laughed "Strange!"
she flushed and barked "Not strange!"
as if I alone had never witnessed
the commonest of rituals.

Brian Bartlett, Underwater Carpentry

And the sister … went and cast herself into the river
and was drowned; and when the [other] sister
perceived this … she also secretly drowned herself.

Palladius, The Book of Paradise (420 A.D.)

GESTURES

Beginning moments before the cessation of a viable heart-
beat, the body becomes a clock. As each minute, hour, day,
week, and month passes, the human body, in death, becomes a
"court-ready" exhibit—a "book," which if read carefully, will
supply critical information answering questions which have, in
the past, remained a mystery.

Robert G. Teather, Encyclopedia of Underwater Investigations

Because beyond their practical function, all gestures have a meaning that exceeds the intention of those who make them; when people in bathing suits fling themselves into the water, it is joy itself that shows in the gesture, notwithstanding any sadness the divers may actually feel. When someone jumps into the water fully clothed, it is another thing entirely: the only person who jumps into the water fully clothed is a person trying to drown; and a person trying to drown does not dive headfirst; he lets himself fall: thus speaks the immemorial language of gestures.

Milan Kundera, Slowness

What does the body of an average drowning victim weigh underwater? How "heavy" is it? These are questions which are often asked. Even the experienced investigator may be under the illusion that a submerged human body is extremely heavy. This misconception is likely nourished by the emotionally charged situation of having to swim to the surface with a body in tow, and is reinforced by the drag felt when a rigor-stiffened, non-streamlined body is moved.

Robert G. Teather, Encyclopedia of Underwater Investigations

A vision returned of the floating woman. Staring downwards into the depths. What did she know, what had she seen?

Michael Köepf, The Fisherman's Son

Like a drowning man who goes down clenching his hands, the way one drowns for failing to stretch out one's body as peacefully as in a bed, in the same way ... but I know.

Georges Bataille, The Impossible

VIATICUM

Yes, there is no good pretending, it is hard to leave everything. The
horror-worn eyes linger abject on all they have beseeched so long,
in a last prayer, the true prayer at last, the one that asks for nothing.
And it is then a little breath of fulfillment revives the dead longings
and a murmur is born in the silent world, reproaching you affec-
tionately with having despaired too late. The last word in the way
of *viaticum*. Let us try it another way. The pure plateau.

Samuel Beckett, Malone Dies

This is a photograph of me.
It was taken some time ago.
At first it seems to be
a smeared
print: blurred lines and grey flecks
blended with the paper;
then, as you scan
it, you see in the left-hand corner
a thing that is like a branch: part of a tree
(balsam or spruce) emerging
and, to the right, halfway up
what ought to be a gentle
slope, a small frame house.
In the background there is a lake,
and beyond that, some low hills.
(The photograph was taken
the day after I drowned.
I am in the lake, in the center
of the picture, just under the surface.
It is difficult to say where
precisely, or to say

how large or small I am:
the effect of water
on light is a distortion
but if you look long enough,
eventually
you will be able to see me.)

Margaret Atwood
This Is a Photograph of Me

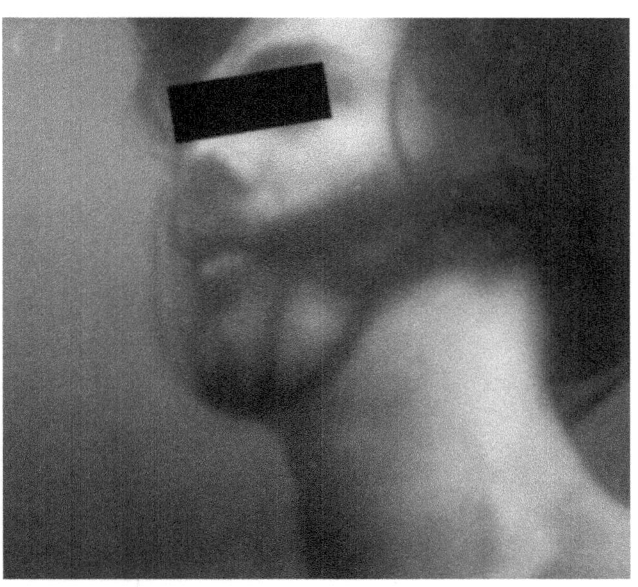

Kamchatka, drowning man not rescued for fear of water-spirit in.

James Fraser, Index to Ovid's Fasti

www.ingramcontent.com/pod-product-compliance
Lightning Source LLC
Chambersburg PA
CBHW050442200726
48295CB00024B/941